LUC

WOLVES OF THE RISING SUN #3

KENZIE COX

Published by Bayou Moon Press, LLC, 2015.

Luc: WOLVES OF THE RISING SUN #3
First edition.

Written by Kenzie Cox.

Join the Packs of the Mating Season

The mating moon is rising…

Wherever that silver light touches, lone male werewolves are seized by the urge to find their mates. Join these six packs of growly alpha males (with six-packs!) as they seek out the smart, sassy women who are strong enough to claim them forever.

The "Mating Season" werewolf shifter novellas are brought to you by six authors following the adventures of six different packs. Each novella is the story of a mated pair (or trio!) with their Happily Ever After. Enjoy the run!

Learn more at thematingseason.com

LUC: WOLVES OF THE RISING SUN

She's gotten under his skin…

Arianna Simms isn't looking for anything permanent. Her two week vacation has everything she needs—her best friend, a quiet bayou town, and the sexy shifter who fills her every desire. He's everything she thinks she wants…until she realizes just exactly how dangerous his world can be.

Luc Riveaux has closed his heart. Some wounds run too deep. But when the gorgeous model from New Orleans starts sharing his bed, something shifts. She's the one person who's managed to break past his barriers. Now he has a choice to make—chase after her and claim her as his or let her go forever.

Sign up for Kenzie's newsletter at www.kenziecox.com. Do you prefer text messages? Sign up for text alerts! Just text SHIFTERSROCK to 24587 to register.

CHAPTER 1
ARIANNA

THE SOUTHERN SUN beat down on Luc's flexing muscles, sending my thoughts to dirty places. Places I'd been only an hour ago. In Luc's shower, his hands and lips driving me insane. I could still feel his hard body claiming mine as the water sluiced over both of us.

Luc straightened and turned deliberately as if he could hear what I was thinking.

I licked my lips.

His twitched and he watched me as he leaned down over the dock, untying the rope holding the airboat. "Like what you see?"

I gave him a coy smile. "You'll do."

A week ago, my life had taken a sudden left turn. Or maybe I'd slipped into an alternate reality. Because seriously… whoever thought that werewolf shifters actually existed outside of the Syfy channel?

Not me, that's for sure. And I'd grown up on the wrong side of the tracks where crime and drugs were a way of life. I'd thought nothing could shock me. I'd been wrong.

Luc grinned, and his eyes glinted with amused trouble. "Ready for this?"

"Sure." A light breeze drifted from the water as I climbed onto the airboat. Sitting in the back row, I turned sideways, more interested in my shifter than I was the sights of the bayou. The landscape was stunning with the Spanish moss, cypress trees, and an abundance of wildlife, but Luc was just plain gorgeous. Dark hair, brilliant green eyes, and a body that sent my hormones into overdrive.

"You're going to miss all the sights if you don't stop staring at my chest," he said, a light chuckle in his tone.

"Who cares?" He'd stripped his T-shirt off nearly the moment we stepped outside. Can't say I blamed him. It was only April, but in southeast Louisiana the heat and humidity were already nearing sauna levels. I gazed up at him through my lashes and gave him a seductive smile.

"Christ, Arianna. Look at me like that one more time and I'm going to carry you back into the house and torture you with my mouth until you're begging me to fuck you."

Everything heated. Goddamn, that was sexy. He'd do it too. It had taken me a few days to get over the shock of learning he was a shifter, but the attraction between us had proved to be too big of a force to deny. Before I'd even decided how I felt about dating a shifter, I'd found myself back in his bed, enjoying every delicious moment of it. Not that we were dating exactly. More like we were friends with *all* the benefits.

"That sounds awfully tempting. Maybe after you finally give me a tour of your family property."

He nodded, but the hunger lurking in his expression only intensified as he let his gaze sweep down to my exposed cleavage. I was wearing a cotton wraparound dress that hugged me in all the right places. Perhaps I was a little overdressed for an airboat ride.

Luc leaned over and caught my lips with his. And when his hand cupped my breast, sending tiny shocks everywhere, I decided I'd worn the exact right thing.

When he finally broke away, we were both a

little winded.

"Umm," I said. "Maybe we should get going before we get too distracted."

He ran his fingers down the back of my neck, sending tingles down my spine, and said, "I'm already distracted. And if I hadn't made you come twice this morning, I'd have you back in my bed right now."

Heat burned my cheeks and I grinned, remembering his morning greeting, his long hard body pressed up against mine, his fingers gently exploring every inch of me until I'd been so wet and ready—

The engine kicked over on the airboat, startling me out of my lust haze. Scenery. Bayou. Gators. Right. I'd asked for this tour of their wildlife sanctuary.

Luc winked at me and guided the boat out into the bayou beneath the tree canopy. He maneuvered slowly at first until he got out into the middle of the waterway, then without much warning, he gunned it. The pungent smell of damp mud and moss was washed away in the wind as we slid out of the trees and into an open swamp area full of water hyacinths, tall grasses, and blooming wildflowers.

The flat-bottomed boat glided over the thick vegetation with ease and back into another canopy of trees. The ride was fascinating and gorgeous, and had I been driving the boat, I'd have been completely lost. The bayou was a maze of waterways and a wild landscape unlike any I'd ever seen before. Utterly fascinating in a creepy sort of way.

Wild, just like the Riveauxs.

Luc slowed the boat, idling near a decaying structure that was being reclaimed by the bayou. "This used to belong to my grandfather, but it was destroyed by Hurricane George in the 1940s. That's when he finally had no choice but to move and join the rest of his pack where we are now."

"It's really secluded," I said.

Luc chuckled. "Yeah. The only way in and out is by boat. The stories of Francis Riveaux are legendary. Total recluse for most of his life."

His expression shifted and his brow furrowed as a slight frown claimed his lips.

That was a sudden change in mood. "Why?"

"Hmm?"

"Why was he a recluse?" I asked.

His expression smoothed. "Oh, he hadn't met his mate. When Sally Ann came along, everything changed. She was a social butterfly. Knew everyone. She's the one who started the bar actually. And he had no choice but to go along with it. The story is he fought her on everything, but she was relentless and eventually he always caved."

I laughed. "She sounds amazing."

"She was." He nodded toward the structure. "Want to check it out?"

I glanced at my canvas tennis shoes, grateful I hadn't worn my sandals, but still, I was wearing a dress and my legs were bare. "I'm not sure I'm dressed correctly for a romp in the wilds of the bayou."

"You're fine. Follow me, and I'll make a trail with my boots."

I sucked in a breath. "What if there are snakes or gators?"

He held up a shotgun. "I've got you covered."

"All right, but I'd feel better if I'd worn jeans."

He maneuvered the airboat over to the embankment, jumped out, and tied the boat to a metal stake already positioned in the ground. "Come on." He held out his hand. "I'll protect you."

"You better."

Luc tightened his grip around my hand, tugged me close, and said, "This place is covered in years of wolf scent. Because of that, animals usually don't stick around long. Our scent acts as a repellent."

Well, he was a predator after all. The familiar thrill of anticipation shot through me straight to my core. Damn. Why did that excite me so much? I was going to need to analyze that one later.

Luc walked in front of me, still holding my hand in his, and led us around to the back of the old homestead, pointing out different forms of vegetation: an old fire pit they'd used when they were kids on campouts, the decaying outhouse, and the bullet holes in the side of an old rotten fence from when they'd all learned to shoot.

"You spent a lot of time here as a kid, didn't you?" I asked.

"Yeah." He stopped and once again trailed his fingers down the back of my neck. He did it almost unconsciously, like it soothed him to touch me. "Our dad used to like to come out here. But after he passed, it was too hard. And now we're so busy with the bar and the gator tours it doesn't get much attention. We probably should do something about the cabin, but there's something sort of symbolic about the bayou claiming it."

I gave him a confused look. "Symbolic?"

He glanced down at me. "The men in our family live and die at the hands of the bayou. It's been the way we make our living for generations. And once one of us goes, we're reclaimed by the earth." He gestured to the land behind us and the cabin. "The family cemetery is back there."

"Really?" I craned my neck, trying to get a glimpse of the tombs. "Can we take a look?"

His expression turned stormy, and I quickly backtracked. "I'm sorry. I didn't mean to intrude. We don't have to go. I—"

He held up his hand. Taking a deep breath, he shook his head. "It's fine. It's just that I haven't been there in a while."

I slipped my arm around his waist. "I understand. That was insensitive. I shouldn't have asked. Ready to go back?"

He gazed over my head and toward the cemetery. There was an intensity to him I hadn't seen since the night he'd told me he was a shifter.

"Luc? You okay?"

He stroked my neck again, still distracted. "Yeah, I think I'd like to talk to Dad for a minute." His features softened and he added, "Introduce you to him."

"Sure," I said and smiled up at him, hoping to lighten the mood a touch. "Just as long as you don't mean meeting in the literal sense. I mean, werewolf is one thing, but if Dad's a vampire or zombie, that might be too much for me."

He laughed, and I felt a small weight lift off my chest. "No. Not literally. Unless he's gone ghost on us, then all bets are off."

It was my turn to laugh. "Got it. Okay. Lead on, wolf boy. I guess now is as good a time as any to meet the rest of the family."

Luc took the lead, stomping down the overgrown vegetation with his boots and keeping an eye out for any wildlife. But he was right. Aside from the few birds high in the trees, there wasn't even so much as a rustle in the grass. Just me and Luc and the harsh spring sun.

CHAPTER 2

LUC

WHAT AN IDIOT I was. Why had I brought Arianna here of all places? Grandfather's camp was a place of family memories infused with love and pain. Memories and nightmares. It's where my father had gone to mourn after my mother had left and where he'd gone to die.

And here I was, sharing the place I loved and hated the most with a woman I'd only known a week.

Why?

I knew the answer. But admitting it would

mean tearing down the solid walls I'd built years before. I gave myself a mental shake.

Snap out of it, man. Christ.

It didn't have to mean anything. Arianna was leaving at the end of the week anyway to go home to New Orleans. Then everything would go back to normal.

We stepped through a small thicket of trees and the cemetery came into view. A dozen or so raised tombs graced the property, the sun baking down on their rough cement tops.

"Wow," she breathed and squeezed my hand as if I needed comfort.

I didn't. The same cold indifference I always felt when I came here settled around my heart.

"It's so nicely kept. I wasn't expecting that based on the state of the old cabin." She stepped forward, studying the list of names etched on Grandfather's tomb.

"Jace keeps the grounds," I said, hearing the flatness in my tone.

She glanced back, her big eyes going soft with pity.

Dammit. That was the last thing I needed. I averted my gaze, staring at the tomb beside Grandfather's. Something wasn't right. A sizeable chunk had cracked off the right corner. Crouching, I studied it and ran my fingers over the damage. "This is new."

Arianna bent down beside me. "You think your brother accidentally hit it with something?"

I shook my head. "No way. Jace would tell us. Besides, all he brings out here is a Weed Eater and some small hand tools. Unless he was taking a hammer to this, it's unlikely he was the cause."

Standing up, I ran a hand through my hair.

"Has to be trespassers." The words came out almost as a growl. This was our family's cemetery. Sacred ground for us. What the hell was anyone doing on our land?

Arianna drifted away, probably unconsciously sensing my wolf clawing right at the surface.

Protect.

The word seized me from deep in my soul.

Family.

My wolf was taking over.

Intruder.

The shift seized me. It was uncontrollable. A powerful force hit me, one I hadn't felt since that day we'd found my father's lifeless body. And just like that day, I shifted, unable to keep my wolf caged.

"Luc!" I heard Arianna call.

But it was too late. I was already in wolf

form, the sour scent of trespassers filling my senses. Turning my head in the direction of their trail, I sniffed the air, let out a long howl, and ran. My paws barely hit the earth as I flew toward my enemy, one goal in mind—protect the family land.

"Luc!" The woman's voice was fainter now. I no longer consciously knew who she was, only that I trusted her. She was not a threat.

Overgrown vegetation caught in my fur and scraped at my legs. With each step, the scent grew stronger, right along with my determination. Then suddenly I broke free of the trees and into an area that had been cleared. Rows and rows of cultivated marijuana plants were thriving right there in the middle of the large island.

I skidded to a stop, sending a clump of dirt and rocks flying forward, followed by a loud snap of steel on steel.

I froze, my body hunched low to the ground, every sense on high alert.

Bear trap.

There it was, a foot in front of me. If I'd taken just a few more steps, I'd have been skewered between those deadly jaws. A shudder ran through me.

"Luc!" Arianna, completely winded, burst through the trees.

I leaped, landing right in front of her, letting out a warning howl. The bear trap had snapped me back to myself, out of my wolf trance.

Her eyes went wide with fear and her hands came up and out as if to silently signal me to calm down.

I jerked my head toward the plants and then took a tentative step forward, trying to let her know I was only protecting her.

Realization dawned in her dark eyes and she

dropped her hands. "Holy shit."

I turned and scanned the area, keeping my nose to the ground. In wolf form, I had a better sense of smell. Nothing moved. There was no sound. Just the stale scent of unfamiliar human. No one else was here. Not now.

Satisfied we were alone, I closed my eyes and concentrated. My bones elongated, cracked, and reformed quickly as I shifted back into a man.

Arianna didn't say anything at first. She just stared at me, her gaze never sweeping over my naked form. No, she was studying me as if trying to see into my mind. I opened my mouth to speak, but she waved her hand toward the crop and asked, "Is this your farm?"

"Excuse me?" I asked, totally caught off guard.

"The marijuana. Is this how you and your brothers make a living?"

"What?" I barked out a startled laugh. "You've got to be joking."

She crossed her arms over her chest and raised one eyebrow. "You didn't answer the question."

"Christ, Arianna. No. Is that what you think of us?"

"I… No. But you have to understand—"

"And if on some wildly off chance it was, do you really think I'd shift and then lure you out here? Why would I do that?"

She shrugged. "I don't know. Maybe you thought someone was stealing your crop. You did go kind of crazy back there. I mean, it's not like you chose to shift, right? Skye told me that sometimes happens if one of you gets super protective or threatened."

I took a deep breath and shook off my incredulity, willing myself to calm down. "Yes.

Skye's correct. We do shift when we get protective. I sensed a foreign human scent. A couple of them. It was strong enough that I thought they might still be here. They aren't, obviously, but they'll be back. No one plants this much herb and doesn't come back for it."

"That's right." All the suspicion in her expression vanished, replaced by naked fear. "And that's why we have to get out of here."

"Whoa," I said, holding my hands out to settle her down just as she had with me. "Everything's okay. No one else is here right now." I took a step to the right, trying to get a glimpse past a row of the plants.

Arianna grabbed my arm, stopping me. "No. This place is probably full of all kinds of traps. These people use everything from homemade land mines to rigged rifles. We have to go. Now."

I pointed over to the bear trap lying a few feet away. "That came close to taking a leg off."

Her eyes went even wider. Then she straightened, appearing to grow a couple of inches taller. "Oh my God." She finally let herself take a look at my body as if checking for any wounds. When she finally looked up, there was relief shining back at me. "You're very lucky, you know."

I nodded. The sound of the jaws snapping still rang in my ears.

"Come on." She tugged on my arm, pulling me back into the trees. "You have to let the sheriff handle this."

That wasn't going to happen. I was ninety-nine percent sure I knew who had planted the illegal cannabis. Skye's ex belonged to an organization called the Hunters—an anti-shifters hate group—and right before she left him, she'd found evidence he was laundering marijuana money for them through his accounting business. It also explained why Lannister had made a bogus claim that one of his relatives had rights to our land and tried to sue us for it. He'd fought so hard over the past year, but the judge finally threw the case out. All the signs pointed to Lannister and his associates being at the center of this shit storm.

And the fuckers had evidence about our shifting abilities. If we called the authorities, they'd out us everywhere. We couldn't let that happen.

If they hadn't been so careless as to traipse through our family cemetery, we might never have known the crop was there. No one would. It was a perfect spot to keep the cannabis hidden.

Once I told Jace and Aiden what we'd found,

we'd call in a couple of buddies and form a plan to clear the land of the plants and whatever other traps they'd left for us.

Then we'd deal with the Hunters ourselves.

Arianna and I didn't speak on our way back to the boat. When we got there, I pulled a spare T-shirt and jeans from a compartment near the driver's seat. We shifters rarely went anywhere without an extra change of clothes. My other set was behind the old homestead, shredded after my unexpected shift.

Arianna climbed on the boat and swept her gaze over me, smiling her secret smile. "Too bad. I was getting used to watching you walk around naked."

I grinned at her. "Tonight. I promise to strip down and you can take your fill as long as you like."

"Count on it."

CHAPTER 3
ARIANNA

LUC SPED THROUGH the bayou, taking half as much time to get back as he had on the way out. But instead of tying up near his house, he pulled up to the dock near the bar. Jace and Aiden were working outside, cutting boards to rebuild the side of the bar that had burned a week ago. They both stopped and stared at us.

Jace cut the motor to his chop saw and raised his eyebrows in question. "Hey, what are you two doing here?" He straightened and turned to Luc, concern suddenly flashing in his eyes. "What happened?"

"Yeah," Aiden added. "What's got you so wound up?"

I glanced between Luc and his brothers, trying to see what they did. Earlier, I could tell Luc was upset, but now he seemed completely normal. The tension had left his shoulders and his face was mostly just… blank.

"It's a pack thing," Luc said in my ear. "My wolf's uneasy and they sense it."

"Oh." As strange as that was, a twinge of jealousy sparked through me. I'd never been that close with anyone. Not even my brother, the one person I'd trust with my life. He'd do anything for me, but neither of us would claim to understand the other. He'd chosen a life of crime, while I'd left all that behind the day I'd graduated high school.

I craved normalcy. A quiet life away from the violence and corruption.

"Let's go inside," Luc said to his brothers and led us into the old bar known as Wolves of the Rising Sun.

"Hi, you two." Skye, Jace's mate, waved. She was sitting at a table doing some paperwork while Rayna, Aiden's mate, was busy painting a freshly Sheetrocked wall. Even though the fire had been in the kitchen, the smoke and water damage had meant the customer area needed a serious remodel. Once the walls were done, they were moving on to the floors.

I went straight for the mini fridge under the bar and pulled out a bottle of water.

Skye followed me, but instead of water, she grabbed three bottles of beer.

"They might need something stronger," I said.

Her eyebrows shot up. "What happened?"

I waved to Luc and his brothers, now sitting

at Skye's table. "Luc's about to tell them."

She pointed to a full whiskey bottle. "Better take that and some shot glasses."

"I got it," Rayna said, joining us.

Together, armed with liquid reinforcement, we joined the men.

Jace glanced at the whiskey. "It's that bad?"

Luc nodded. "Arianna and I took a detour over to Grandfather's place."

"You did?" Rayna said, shock written all over her pretty face. "What—" She noted Luc's sudden stormy expression and then cleared her throat. "I mean, that's good."

He gave her a flat stare that clearly said she should mind her own business.

It didn't faze her though. She smiled sweetly. "Continue."

That twinge of jealousy was back. Not because I was jealous of Rayna. I knew nothing was going on between them. Rayna and Aiden were mated. This had everything to do with that connection they shared. The one that made them able to communicate without even speaking.

I spent the next few minutes lost in my own thoughts as Luc explained what we'd found. It wasn't until I heard Aiden say, "Tomorrow we'll get up early and go clear the area," that I snapped out of my haze.

"No. You can't do that," I said. "It's way too dangerous."

Luc covered my hand with his. "Arianna. We—"

"No." I jumped up, my heart nearly pounding out of my chest. "Have any of you ever been around pot farmers? Do you know what they're capable of? You already know they set traps. These people are dangerous. They'll make your lives hell if you do this. Trust me. I've seen this before."

The entire room was silent as they all stared at me. Heat crawled up my neck.

Shit. Shit. Shit. Nice outburst, Arianna.

But I stood tall, my shoulders back. A little embarrassment was worth it if they'd just leave the grow site to the authorities.

"Ari." Skye reached out and touched my arm lightly. "There's a problem with that plan."

"What's that?" I lowered myself back down to the chair.

"We know who's growing. Right before I left Lannister, I found out he'd been laundering money for a pot dealer."

"And you think whoever's responsible for this crop is that dealer?"

"Yes," Luc said. "Lannister also filed a bull-shit lawsuit to try to take the property. We never knew why, but now we do. There is every reason to believe he and his associates are behind this."

I tightened my fingers around my bottle of water. "Okay. I always thought Lannister was shady. But why not just call the police? I don't get it."

Luc touched his shoulder. The one that had the bullet scar I'd seen dozens of times over the past week. "He's the one who shot me. And he also has a video of Jace shifting. If we cause problems for them, they'll turn it over to the press."

All the fight went out of me, and I sank back into my chair. The implications of what he'd said hit me hard. Shifters lived in secret, always avoiding the public eye. If it got out they were here, they'd have to move, change their names, leave everything they knew. Their land, their heritage, their community. It wasn't an option.

"So they're blackmailing you. Why stop there?" I asked, my voice flat.

"I have proof they're laundering," Skye said. "If they go public, so will I. And if we bring in the cops, it's a violation of the agreement we made."

I glanced at Luc. He nodded, confirming what she'd said.

"So you're screwed. And as long as that crop is there, you're all in danger of being prosecuted. If the authorities did find it, you'd be liable," I said, thinking out loud.

"I suppose we would," Jace said. "That's why we need to get rid of it and scour the property for any more hidden farms."

The rest of the pack joined in the discussion as they formed a plan to dispose of the marijuana. I sat quietly beside Luc, images of my childhood running through my mind. Guns.

Violence. Instability. The old fear and desperation hit me hard, and all I could see was my mother lying on the side of the road in a pool of blood.

I stood on shaky legs. "I need some air."

Luc's chair scraped against the wooden floor as he stood and put his arm around my waist. "Arianna? Are you all right?"

The concern in his tone nearly broke me. "Fine," I forced out, willing my voice to stay strong. Now wasn't the time to lose my shit. "Just need a second."

"We'll be right back," Luc told the others and guided me out the front door.

Once we were on the porch, I leaned against a post on the railing and stared out at the deserted parking lot.

Luc stood behind me, his hands resting lightly on my hips. "It's going to be fine. We've suffered through worse than this."

I sucked in a breath and let it out slowly. "Like when you were shot?"

"Well, yeah." His breath tickled my neck. "But I'm a shifter. We can endure a lot more than the average man."

I closed my eyes and shook my head. "You're not immortal."

He tightened his hold on me, pulling me back so that I was leaning against him. "You're right. I'm not. But my world is dangerous. It's just a fact of life for us. Even if Lannister and his ilk went away today, someone else would step in, determined to cause us trouble. It's been that way for centuries, Ari."

"So it's just a way of life then?" I glanced over my shoulder and tilted my head up, meeting his intense eyes. "You're constantly on edge, always on guard in case some asshole threatens the pack?"

"Pretty much. Most days things are calm. But I'm always on full alert. I have to be."

I nodded, my heart sinking. I couldn't do this. Couldn't be around this type of life, even if they were the good guys. I'd lived in constant fear. I wouldn't do it again.

Luc pressed his lips to my neck, giving me a whisper of a kiss. It was so tender my heart nearly broke in two. No one made me feel the way he did.

Treasured and safe. He was strong and capable, would put himself between me and any threat. I was sure of it. That should be enough. If I was anyone else, it probably would be. The problem was me. I couldn't let go of my deep-seated fears.

I twisted in his arms. "Would it be too much trouble to take me back to your house? I'm really tired and could use a break while you talk with your brothers."

"Sure." He bent his head and brushed his lips over mine. "I'll get Aiden's keys and be right back."

When we pulled up to his house, I sat there in the idling truck, not sure what to say. I was supposed to stay for another week, but now I knew that wasn't an option. I had to leave today.

"I'll be back in a few hours," Luc said, tucking a lock of hair behind my ear. "Then I'll make you dinner."

"Really?" I gazed up at him, getting lost in his dark blue eyes. "You cook?"

He laughed. "Sure. Don't you?"

I shook my head. "No. Not unless it involves reheating leftovers and takeout."

Leaning in so close that our lips were almost touching, he whispered, "Well then, tonight I'll make you gumbo."

"Sounds yummy."

"Not half as yummy as dessert." Then he pressed his lips to mine, his kiss full of passion and a promise of more to come. "Two hours. I'll be back."

"I'll be here," I said without thinking and climbed out of the truck.

And as I watched him head back to the bar, my heart sank and a blanket of sadness overwhelmed me. I knew I should pack up and leave right then. Should walk inside, throw my clothes in my suitcase, and drive off, never looking back.

But I couldn't. He'd promised gumbo. And a night filled with passion.

Tomorrow. First thing. I'd go then.

CHAPTER 4

LUC

THE HAUNTED LOOK in Arianna's eyes was burned in my brain. Her expression when we'd been standing on the porch at the bar had made me want to gather her in my arms and keep her safe forever.

It had killed me to leave her at my house and head back to the bar. I hadn't had a choice though. Ignoring the grow site wasn't an option.

I drummed my fingers on the table, listening to Jace and Aiden finalize the plan. At daybreak the three of us, along with a couple of Jace's Army buddies, would head to the island, armed to the hilt. Jace and his crew had combat training. They'd be able to suss out any land mines and other traps. Then over the next few days, we'd chop the plants down and dispose of them.

"Here." Rayna handed me a longneck. "You look like you could use a drink."

"Thanks." I took the beer but didn't drink it.

"Is Arianna all right?" Her dark eyes were filled with concern.

I shrugged. "Honestly, I don't know. She seemed pretty spooked by everything."

Rayna nodded. "It's a lot to process in a short time."

I let out a sigh and closed my eyes. "Yeah."

"I'm sure she'll get used to it. It didn't take Skye long." She tilted her head toward Jace's girl. She'd gone back to the insurance paperwork she was filling out for us.

"That's different. They knew each other a

long time."

Rayna snorted. "Barely."

"She also has a thing for real wolves."

She nodded. "I'll give you that. It probably made the transition easier. But don't worry. It's clear you and Arianna have a connection. She's not going anywhere."

I let the beer bottle drop on the table and pushed it away. "She's leaving in six days, Ray. Don't let your imagination run away with you. She's not my mate."

One of her perfect eyebrows arched. "You sure about that?"

"Yes." I stood and turned toward my brothers sitting at the next table. "I'm headed home. See you in the morning."

They mumbled disinterested good-byes as my work boots echoed off the old floors.

When I got outside, I scowled, remembering

I needed to take the airboat back to my dock. It was an extra fifteen minutes by boat than it was truck. The added time irritated me. All I wanted right then was Arianna. Naked. And underneath me, scoring my shoulders with her sharp nails until I made her purr with contentment. And then I wanted to hold her in my arms all night, taking in her sweet vanilla scent.

By the time I slid the boat up to the dock at my house, the sun was already going down and a purplish sunset lit the sky. I smiled to myself, took the front steps two at a time, and barreled into the house.

Music wafted from an iPod dock stationed on my kitchen counter. An open bottle of wine and two glasses sat together next to it, along with a small plate of cheese, salami, and crackers.

"I thought you might want a snack," Arianna said from my coffee-colored couch, appearing to be wearing just a robe and nothing else.

All of the tension of the day washed away. Seeing her relaxing in my house, completely at home, felt… right. As if she belonged there.

Mine.

The word flashed in my mind, and I felt it resonate deep inside my gut. Something I'd never felt with anyone. Not even with Rayna, my best friend, who'd shared my house for five years. This was completely different. And to my surprise, completely welcome.

I smiled, poured us both a glass of wine, and brought the tray over to the couch as I sat next to her. "Thanks."

She took a sip. "You're welcome."

Her bronze skin glowed in the soft lighting, and she looked so soft and lovely I promptly put down my wineglass and pulled her into my arms. "How hungry are you?"

She gazed up at me, her eyes intense. "For food? Not at all."

"How about for this?" I slid my hand up her neck and dipped my head, brushing my lips over her cheek until I stopped just short of her lips.

"Starving," she breathed and closed the distance. Her hands fisted in my T-shirt as she pulled me closer, her tongue darting over mine.

I tightened my arms around her, taking my time tasting her, my movements slow and deliberate. Tonight I wanted to explore every inch of her gorgeous body and savor everything she had to offer.

Arianna broke the kiss and brought one hand up, tracing a finger over my jawline. "Should we take this to the bedroom?"

I ran my hand up her bare thigh, stopping

just before I reached her center. "Yes, we should."

"Oh God," she breathed and rested her head against the couch.

I chuckled. "Or we can stay right here."

She gave me a tiny nod and bent her knee, giving me access to her incredible heat.

"You're not wearing any panties," I said, scraping my teeth over her neck, resisting the urge to bite her. To make her mine.

She moaned as I pressed my fingers against her slick flesh. "More," she murmured.

I shook my head. "Not yet. You're not ready."

Her fingers curled around my forearm, and then in one swift movement she twisted and swung around so she was straddling me. "I've been ready for hours."

CHAPTER 5

ARIANNA

THE MOMENT I decided this would be my last night with Luc, I made up my mind that I was going to give us both a night to remember. He'd started this seduction scene so tenderly, as if he wanted to ease me into a night of lovemaking. But I had other plans.

Grinding into his already-hard shaft, I yanked his shirt off and raked my nails down his chest, making him jerk up against me.

"Christ, Ari," he said and then moaned, his eyes smoldering with lust.

The desire pouring off him made me want to

rip his jeans open and ride him right then and there. But it wasn't time yet. Instead, I bent my head and kissed his lower lip while I slowly slid off his lap and kneeled on the floor in front of him.

"Hey," he said softly. "What are you—"

"Shh," I said as I grabbed a pillow and positioned it under my knees. Then I went to work on his button fly.

His abs flexed under my light touch, and I knew I was driving him crazy.

"Come back up here," he said, his voice hoarse. "I want to be touching you... everywhere."

I gave him a saucy smile. "Oh, you will." I worked him free of his jeans and palmed his velvety shaft.

He sucked in a sharp breath.

"After I'm done." Then I bent and tasted his

salty tip.

He buried one hand in my thick hair, barely holding on as he clutched his other hand at his side.

I looked up at him through my lashes. "It's okay to get a little rough."

His blue eyes flashed and he tightened his fist, lightly pulling my hair. It was just enough to send a bolt of heat between my thighs.

"Yes," I whispered. "Just like that.

Then I ran my tongue from base to tip, teasing him, enjoying the hitch in his breath. "Tell me what to do," I ordered.

He let out a strangled groan.

"Say it, Luc."

"Arianna."

"Yes?"

"Wrap your lips around my cock. Now."

I felt his shaft grow even larger in my hand.

Pleasure rippled through me, and my lips curved up into a pleased smile.

"Happy to," I whispered and took him deep.

"Oh God," he said. "That's… fucking amazing."

Still holding him with one hand, I started to move, my mouth working him until he vibrated under my ministrations. His grip on my hair tightened, but instead of pain, all I felt was power. It was a huge turn-on.

My breasts became heavy with need and everything pulsed. I needed him. Needed to feel him inside me.

And then, as if he'd heard my silent plea, he grabbed me by the waist and yanked me up so I was straddling him once more. I hovered above him, our eyes locked.

"Ari," he said, his voice so low I barely heard him.

"Yes?" I whispered, settling myself so that the tip of his cock found my center.

His fingers dug into my hips, and he answered by surging up and pulling me down at the same time. I let out a loud gasp from the shock of him filling me. We stayed locked together for just a moment. But when our eyes met again, we both started to move.

My hands were everywhere. His arms, his back, his chest, his hair. His hard muscles rippled under my exploration, fueling my ever-growing need.

"You're so fucking beautiful," Luc said, tearing my robe off. His hands cupped my breasts, his thumbs rolling over my hardened nipples. And before I could recover from the delicious sensation, his mouth was on me, kissing, scraping, sucking.

"Luc," I gasped out, throwing my head back.

His hands dropped and palmed my ass. He stilled, holding me tight to him as I pulsed around him.

"I need all of you," he said and stood up with me still wrapped around him.

In strong, quick strides, he carried me to his bedroom, only breaking our connection when he lowered me to the bed.

He stood there, staring at me with that intense gaze as he divested himself of the rest of his clothes. He was pure perfection. The wolf symbol tattooed over this heart, the rough bullet-wound scar on his shoulder, his tanned skin, dark hair, and deep blue eyes. I'd never seen anyone more rugged and beautiful at the same time. A small pang stabbed my heart. After tonight, this would only be a memory.

"What's wrong?" Luc asked.

"Nothing," I said, forcing the thoughts from

my mind. Tonight was for us. "You've just got me all wound up. I don't think I can wait any longer."

Spreading my legs, I pressed one hand to my stomach and cupped one breast with the other.

His gaze went straight to my sex, and I lifted my hips in a suggestive movement.

He moved, crawling on the bed until he was over me, his eyes flashing as he buried his head between my legs. His expert tongue darted out, laving just the right spot. I let out a loud cry, a powerful orgasm ripping through me.

My limbs went boneless, and I could barely move as Luc kissed his way up over my stomach, my breasts, and finally my neck.

When he got to my ear, he whispered, "I'm going to spend every night of the next week making you come just like that."

"That sounds like a threat," I said lightly, my

eyes closed.

"It is." His breath ghosted over my skin.

A shiver ran through me, and I let myself pretend everything he said was true. Because I wanted it to be. Needed it to be if only for a short while. "Luc?"

"Yes, love?" he said, his hands exploring my curves.

"Fuck me. Hard. Like you mean it."

He stilled his hands and met my gaze, a wolfish expression on his. "Don't say things like that unless you mean it."

"I mean it. I want you. Now."

A low growl rippled from his throat as he crushed his lips to mine, searing me with his kiss. And then before I could barely respond, he pulled me up and flipped me over onto my hands and knees.

"Are you sure you want this," he said into

my ear from behind me.

"Yes," I said, breathless, trembling with anticipation.

His hands gripped my hips and he slammed into me, filling me so full I gasped out his name.

"Say it again," he said with another powerful thrust.

"Luc!"

"Again."

I did as he demanded and pushed back, meeting his pace.

"That's it, Arianna. You're mine. Tonight you're all mine."

Everything about our lovemaking was wild, out of control, full of dark, almost angry, passion. As if we were trying to take something from each other, to steal a piece of the other's soul. It was all need and sex and sensation. And hot as hell.

Luc quickened his pace and his hands moved to my breasts, squeezing hard. Pleasure and pain mixed, fueling the crescendo building deep inside me. My breath quickened. I felt myself tumbling over the edge of control and welcomed it.

"Harder," I demanded.

Luc tightened his hold once more and pounded into me, quickly pulling out and pushing back in, over and over again, his thrusts punishing and perfect.

"God, yes!" I cried.

Luc released one of my breasts and pressed his thumb to my already-throbbing clit. My muscles suddenly spasmed around him, and with one last thrust, he ground into me, both of us crying out as we orgasmed together.

Afterward, we lay side by side in on Luc's bed. I listened while his breathing grew steadier and deeper. When I was fairly certain he'd fallen asleep, I curled into him, resting my head on his shoulder.

"There you are," he said, his voice groggy with sleep.

I sucked in a short breath, trying to hold back the tears burning the backs of my eyes. My heart stuttered in my chest. Dammit. How was I ever going to survive this?

Luc lazily trailed his fingers over my bare thigh and pressed a soft kiss to my temple. "'Night, Ari," he whispered.

"'Night, Luc," I choked out.

His hand stilled, and a few moments later, a soft snore filled the room.

I lay there beside him, wide awake for what seemed like hours, torturing myself with the decision I'd made. But when he finally rolled over, I steeled myself, slipped out of the bed, and pulled on the clothes I'd left on the nightstand earlier in the day.

Moonlight shone through the window, illuminating the beautiful man before me. "I'll miss you," I whispered and tiptoed out of the room.

CHAPTER 6
LUC

I WOKE WITH one thing on my mind. Arianna. And her soft curves. After the night before, as incredible as it had been, I had big plans for slow, lazy morning sex where I could take my time enjoying the gorgeous woman sharing my bed.

Except the woman in question was MIA.

I eyed the alarm clock on the nightstand. It was early. The sun hadn't even risen yet.

Determined to find her and drag her back to my bed, I got up, checked the bathroom, and then headed into the living area.

Nothing. No lights were on. No Arianna on the couch or on the front porch.

No car.

Her white Honda Pilot was gone.

I tore back into the house, flipping on lights as I went. Her handbag was missing from the table near the door. There were no high-heeled shoes lined up against the wall.

Shit! A ball of frustration rose up in my throat, nearly choking me.

I eyed the bedroom, already knowing what I was going to find. But I went in anyway and opened my closet. The area I'd cleared for her early in the week was completely empty.

Arianna was gone.

I sank down onto the edge of the bed and ran my hands through my hair.

What had happened? Last night had been… Christ. Had it been too much for her? I dismissed the thought as quickly as it'd formed. No. She'd been the instigator in that seduction scene. Had been from the very beginning. She'd been dressed in only a robe, nothing else. Had the wine ready. Not to mention she'd had my dick in her mouth within five minutes of me getting home.

Goddammit. She'd planned it.

And then left me like a fucking one-night stand after practically living together the past week. No note. No number. No address. Just gone.

The old familiar pain and hatred that had poisoned me as a teenager came roaring back, eating away at my gut. And unwanted memories crept back into my consciousness. Aiden and me clutching the railing of the porch as our mother loaded the trunk of her beat-up Mustang, of her glancing over at us, her face hardened with determination. Our father standing at the window watching her go, a bottle of whiskey in his hand. Then the promise that she'd come back for us as soon as she was settled.

She never had.

Fuck.

I shook my head, dislodging the memories, and slammed the door on the unwanted emotions. After pulling on jeans and a T-shirt, I headed for my kitchen. Instead of coffee, I poured a double shot of whiskey and downed it.

The burn of the amber liquid was a welcome reprieve. I poured another and when the glass was empty, the numbness had already started to take over.

The rumble of a truck filtered through the window, but I ignored it. I just didn't give a fuck.

A car door slammed, followed by a knock and Rayna calling, "Luc? Ready?"

I pressed my hands against the counter and bent my head, willing her to go away.

More rapid knocking, followed by the unlocking of the door. Rayna was my best friend and used to live in my house. I instantly regretted not getting my key back.

"Go away, Ray. I'm not in the mood."

"Where's Arianna?" she asked, coming to stand next to me in my kitchen.

"Gone."

"Home?"

I shrugged. "No idea. When I woke up this morning she'd already packed and left."

"Holy shit." She curled her fingers around my arm. "And you didn't know she was leaving?"

I shook my head. "Can we talk about this

later?"

"Sure, but…" She glanced over her shoulder at the door.

"What?"

"Aiden is waiting. We're supposed to go deal with the grow site this morning."

"Christ. I forgot." I fisted my hands, wanting to punch something. My head swam from the whiskey, and I knew if I didn't eat something there'd be hell to pay. "I need breakfast. Go on without me. I'll catch up."

"You sure? I can stay with you." There was worry in her dark eyes.

That pissed me off more. "I'm fine. We barely knew each other. She was supposed to leave early next week anyway. If she didn't want to be here, it was better she go now."

Rayna stepped in front of me, staring up with concern as she slipped her arms around my waist. "I know there's more going on—"

"Ray." I stepped back, dislodging myself from her hold. "I told you. I'm fine. I just need coffee and something to eat."

Her eyes narrowed with slight irritation before they softened. "What I was going to say was I know there's more going on inside you that you won't talk about, but if you need me—for anything—you know I'm here for you."

I closed my eyes, letting her calming presence wash over me.

"Luc," she said softly as she put her arms around me again and hugged me, "it's still okay to let your guard down around me."

My heart twisted. Rayna was the one person who knew me inside and out. There was no point in lying about my mental state. She could tell I'd checked out emotionally. "I know," I said, my voice entirely too rough. I cleared my throat. "We'll talk later."

She squeezed harder, kissed my cheek, and headed for the front door. "I'll tell Aiden you'll be right behind us."

I nodded, considering another shot of whiskey. No. Any more and I might not be functional. Time for food.

Ten minutes later as I was sitting down to plow through my eggs and bacon, my door opened again. Skye poked her head in. Her long blond hair was tied up in a high ponytail, and she was wearing jeans and work boots. "Is it okay if I come in for a minute?"

I raised my eyebrows in question but jerked my head toward the seat next to me. "Sure. I thought you were with Jace out in the bayou already."

The screen door slammed behind her. "We were on our way when Arianna called."

I put my fork down, suddenly not hungry at all. "She did?"

She nodded as she headed for the coffeepot. "She told me she left."

I picked up my mug and took a gulp, scalding my tongue. But I ignored it. "Did she say why?"

Skye sat next to me, holding her full cup. "Not exactly, but I can make a decent guess."

"She doesn't date poor bayou guides?" I asked, ignoring the self-hatred trying to worm its way into my brain.

"Oh, come on, Luc," Skye said, exasperation in her tone. "She's not like that and you know it."

I averted my gaze and picked up my fork again, aware I was being an ass. Arianna had never made me feel like my job was beneath her. It was just easier to place blame somewhere other than myself.

Skye leaned in. "Are you really upset that she left or is this all about a sore ego?"

I glared at her. "What the hell kind of question is that? I'm the one who woke up alone in my bed this morning without even the courtesy of a fucking note. I think I'm entitled to feel however I want to about it."

"You're right," she said, sitting back in the chair. "Except your answer matters to me."

"Why?" Curiosity was softening the walls I'd snapped in place earlier. Skye had something to tell me, and her question was some kind of test.

She reached over and tucked her hand into mine. "Listen, Arianna has some things in her past. Painful things. And if you really care about her, I think I need to tell you. But if you don't and this is all about some male-ego bullshit, then I'd rather keep her confidence. So if you could just answer truthfully, then I'll know how to navigate this."

My walls shattered. She'd been hurt. My wolf stirred, needing to protect her. Pushing the plate away, I turned and gave Skye my full attention. "I didn't want her to leave. This morning when I realized she was gone… Well, old shit came back to haunt me. Whatever I'm feeling, it isn't about my ego."

"I see," she said quietly.

There was no doubt Jace had told her about our family. She probably already had a good idea what was going on with me. There was no need to explain further.

Skye picked up her coffee mug and took a sip. "How much do you know about Arianna's family?"

"Not much. Neither of us brought it up."

"Not surprising. All right. Did you know her

only family is her brother?"

I shook my head. "No parents?"

"None," she confirmed. "Arianna's mother was a single parent. Her dad was never in the picture. I'm not even sure she knows who he is. According to her, they had a modest house in a nice neighborhood, and while there wasn't a lot of money, she never felt like she was missing out on anything. And then when Ari was nine, her mom died in a car accident. Ari was there. She watched her take her last breath."

Jesus. That poor little girl. My heart ached. "Fucking awful."

"It gets worse." Skye stared me straight in the eye. "She had no relatives. No one to take her in. Luc, she was put in the system. The brother she talks about is a foster brother."

"She was only nine years old?" My heart felt like it was cracking. Nothing about Arianna had even hinted at the trauma of her childhood. She was full of life and sass and confidence. Damn. What was hiding beneath her layers?

Skye nodded. "The family she was placed with was trouble."

Adrenaline shot through my veins as the urge to rip someone apart gripped me. "Tell me they didn't… abuse her."

"Oh God. No." Skye reached out and squeezed my arm. "Sorry. Nothing like that. Arianna said when she first got there, her foster parents were okay. She was a mess because her whole life had been shattered. But they were trying. But then the dad lost his job and everything went to shit. They started working with a family member who was heavy in the drug trade and eventually became big-time dealers themselves. She was too afraid to say anything, and by the time she was eighteen, she'd seen unspeakable things."

"How'd she get out?" I ground my teeth together at the thought of what all she must've endured.

"College. She got grants and scholarships and never looked back."

"That's good." But it didn't make up for the injustices of her young life.

"Don't you see? That's why she left. Even though she knows you guys have nothing to do with the grow site, she just can't stomach being around anything to do with the drug world. And although she didn't say it, I suspect she's uncomfortable with the fact we're all shifters and live our lives in the shadow of danger."

I sat very still as I took that in. It was true; our lives were complicated and always under some sort of threat. But we took care of business without breaking any laws… mostly.

"She's scared, Luc." Skye stood up. "I thought you needed to know."

"Goddammit." I brought my fist down on the table. "And now she's a part of this whether she wants to be or not." I glanced up at Skye. "She knows about us. People may have seen her with me. The wrong people. She's a target now."

Skye bit her lower lip, guilt flashing in her eyes. "I know. It's my fault. I'm the one who invited her here. If I—"

"Stop. We're not going to play that game, you hear me? By that logic we could blame Rayna for losing control and shifting in front of her and then me for explaining and telling her the whole truth. What we need to do now is concentrate on keeping her safe."

"But she left. How are we going to do that?"

"I need her address. Do you have it?"

"Sure." Skye pulled out her phone and

scrolled through her contacts. "Want me to text it to you?"

"E-mail."

She tapped on the screen a few times. A second later, I heard the swoosh sound of an e-mail being sent. "There. Now what's your plan?"

"Nothing we need to discuss right now. I've got it covered."

"But—"

"Really." I grabbed her hand and tugged her over to the door. "I've got it covered. Go find Jace. I'll meet you guys at the island shortly."

She hesitated.

"Trust me on this, all right?"

"Fine. But if anything happens to her on your watch, you'll have me to answer to, got it?"

"Loud and clear."

Skye thinned her lips, obviously displeased. I couldn't blame her. I'd have been pissed in her shoes. But if she knew who I planned to call and told Jace, there'd be hell to pay.

I glanced over at my phone sitting on the counter. As much as I didn't want to make the call, I was out of options. Arianna was headed back to New Orleans where she could be a sitting target.

There was no choice.

Arianna was all that mattered.

I crossed the room, snatched up the phone, and dialed.

CHAPTER 7
ARIANNA

FIVE DAYS. THAT'S how long it had been since I'd slipped out of Luc's house, determined to distance myself from him and any legal trouble. I'd only lasted two before I'd made the call to my brother—the high-profile hacker who went by the name of Smoke. It'd taken twenty-four hours, a mile-long list of favors, and a couple of empty threats before I'd finally convinced him to let me hire him.

But he hadn't been happy about it. Downright pissed in fact when I said I'd go to his rival. It was a lie. I wouldn't have. Chances were he knew it too. I wasn't sure why he agreed, but I wasn't asking. It was enough that he'd given in. Only one of the conditions was that I had to do some fieldwork to get to Lannister, the douche bag who'd put that bullet hole in Luc's shoulder.

"Chivas Regal. Eighteen years," I said to the bartender and tried to act as if I didn't notice Lannister sitting three seats down, staring at me. It was likely he was trying to place me, but if I had any luck at all, my dark red wig, green contacts, and out-of-character sexified business suit would throw him off the mark.

"You got it, sweetheart." The handsome middle-aged bartender smiled before turning to pull the whisky bottle from the shelf. In a dark, perfectly pressed suit, he embodied everything the whiskey bar known as the Hidden Flask tried to project. Class. Money. Prestige.

But I knew better. Lannister and his buddies

had bankrolled the place. All of them were criminals who'd only managed to stay out of the system because of family connections and backroom bribes.

The bartender handed me my Chivas Regal, and I took a small sip to settle my nerves. It didn't help. Neither had walking around the block five times before I'd finally found the courage to get down to business. Sucking in a breath, I turned to find Lannister staring at my chest.

Good. That was the plan.

"Well, hello there, darlin'," he drawled as if he was a Southern gentleman. He wasn't. His family went back generations in Louisiana, but he was far from anything anyone would call gentlemanly.

"Hi," I said shyly and leaned in just a touch so he'd get a better view of my goods.

His lips turned up into a slimy smile that made my skin crawl. God, he was the worst kind of creepy. The kind of guy who wore multiple personalities. It's how he'd fooled Skye for so long before she finally saw through to his true colors.

"Looks like you're going to need another drink soon."

I glanced at my mostly untouched glass and reminded myself not to roll my eyes. "It would appear so."

He raised a hand to signal the bartender. Then he gestured to me and pointed to my drink, indicating I was ready for round two. Right. Like I was even going to finish the first one.

Lannister raised his glass and eyed me, this time meeting my eyes. "I know you from somewhere."

Dammit! If he put two and two together, this shit show was going to go up in flames in about five seconds flat. "Maybe," I said coyly. "I've done a few cameos in the film industry."

His smile turned almost gleeful as he scanned my body again. "Right. An actress. Of course. With a body like that, what else would you be doing?"

Relief mingled with disgust and made me nauseated. He'd bought it, thank God. But the way he was looking at me... Every fiber of my being told me to get the hell away from him. And quick. But I couldn't. Not yet. I forced a smile and took the tiniest sip of my whisky and longed to down the entire contents. But if I was going to get what I came for, I couldn't afford to be even slightly tipsy.

"What have I seen you in?" he asked and slid over to sit on the stool next to me.

I dropped my hand to his wrist and trailed my fingers up his forearm. "It's no fun if I have to tell you, is it?"

His gaze stayed trained on my fingers. Then he grabbed my hand in his and climbed off the stool. "No it isn't. Let's get out of here, shall we?"

My flight instinct kicked in, and I had to fight to not instantly pull away. Everything was going exactly according to plan. All I had to do was keep him occupied while my brother did his thing. "Dinner?"

"We can order in," he said, tugging me toward the front door.

I gritted my teeth and followed. But as soon as we were standing on Magazine Street, I slipped my arm through his and leaned in, glancing up at him with my lips formed into a pout. "Do you think we could stop for appetizers or something? I haven't eaten, and I really don't think I can wait."

He let his gaze fixate on my chest again.

Fucking pig.

"Yeah, doll. There's a place a couple of blocks down that serves oysters."

I bent my head and nodded just to keep him from seeing the disgust in my expression. Of course oysters. But mission accomplished. "Perfect."

Lannister, whom I noted hadn't even asked my name yet, slipped his arm around my waist and let his hand drop to my ass.

I stiffened and gave him a sharp look.

"What's wrong, doll? I thought that's what you were offering back at the bar." His almost-black eyes narrowed as he studied me entirely too intently.

Warning bells went off in my head. There

was no room for him to be second-guessing anything. I turned into him and placed my hand flat on his chest. Then I gazed up at him through my lashes, smiling shyly. "It is what I'm offering. I just wasn't expecting to get started so soon."

His hand tightened on my ass as his features turned heated.

Christ. I was never going to make it through this.

He chuckled and jerked his head. "The oysters are this way. Unless you've changed your mind and you're ready to wrap those long caramel legs around me right now. I know a place—"

I held up a hand. "Food first. Then we can play."

"Right." His hand moved to my lower back, and together we walked the two blocks to a rustic seafood bistro.

The moment he let me go to slide into our

booth, relief rushed through me. Being touched by him was positively vile. I took my seat across from him and smiled up at the hostess. "What's good here?"

Lannister jumped in before she could answer. "We're having oysters. Raw. We'll start with two dozen and go from there."

I fixed him with an irritated stare, but he was too busy trying to impress the waitress with his knowledge of wines.

"Do you have any private reserves from the Napa region? Nothing from the central valley or the coastal regions."

She raised one eyebrow and glanced around. The old restaurant was bustling, but it was far from a white tablecloth kind of place. "We have house red or white. Otherwise we have local beers on tap."

Lannister scowled, shoved his menu at her,

and said, "The red. But I want to taste it first."

She nodded and glanced at me.

"White please." I wouldn't be around long enough to drink it, but no need to raise suspicion. "And water."

"Of course." The waitress nodded and scurried away.

Lannister kept his gaze trained on her ass until she disappeared behind the bar. Then he turned to me and cocked his head. "So, sweetheart, what's your name?"

It was about time. "Karen."

"Seriously?" He gave me a disbelieving look and snorted. "That seems pretty plain for a girl like you... I was expecting something a little more exotic."

Anger boiled in my chest, and I knew there was no way I was going to be able to keep my expression neutral. I had no qualms with being called exotic. Being Creole and Spanish had given me caramel skin; dark, unruly hair; and a curvaceous build. But the way he'd said the words "a girl like you" made my skin crawl. As if I was a fetish or something.

"Hey, relax, Karen," he said, his lips curled into his signature predatory smile. "I don't care what your name is."

No shit. I carefully rearranged my face, hiding my anger. "Glad to hear it."

He nodded and pulled his phone out.

I glanced over and spotted our waitress coming back with our drinks. Now was my chance.

"Do you think I could use your phone for just a moment?" I asked him. "I forgot mine and I need to let my roommate know I've made other plans. We were supposed to meet later."

"Roommate?" He palmed his phone and

stared at me with renewed interest. "Is she the adventurous type? Maybe she'd like to join us?"

Oh son of a... What a tool. "Maybe. I can check if she's up for it."

He punched in his code to unlock his phone and handed it to me. "Tell her I have enough stamina for an entire harem."

Charming. He must've worked extremely hard to keep this version of himself hidden from Skye. She'd have dumped him in two seconds flat.

I smiled and took the phone from him, holding it in my lap where the table shielded it from his view. And while I watched him watch the waitress, I slipped the small charger-like device out of my pocket and plugged it into the phone. Typing faster than a speed demon, I sent my brother a message letting him know I was in.

He texted back right away. *Give me forty-five*

seconds.

"Here you are," our waitress said, unloading my glass of water and the two wineglasses. She handed the glass to Lannister, waiting.

He took a long swig, drinking nearly half the glass, and then nodded. "This will do."

Wine connoisseur, my ass. He might as well have drunk it straight from the bottle.

"Your oysters will be here in just a moment," the waitress said, shaking her head as she stalked off.

"Hurry," Lannister said, not looking at her. He was studying me. His gaze was so intense I was sure he was going to place me. Realize we'd met at one of Skye's parties when they'd been together. Before she'd mated with Jace and turned were.

"Well?" he asked. "Is she up for it?"

"She's considering it," I said.

He held out his hand. "Let me talk to her."

Oh, dammit. "Hold on. She's asking me something." I typed *Hurry!*

Ten more seconds.

"Karen," Lannister drawled, a hint of irritation in his tone. "I just want a chance to woo her with my considerable charms."

I softened my features and gave him my best pouty expression. "I'm talking her into it. Trust me. She's slow to warm up, but when she does... Whoa, look out. Feisty, that one. We just can't scare her off."

The phone pinged. *Got it.*

With my heart nearly pounding out of my chest, I pulled the charger-like device from the phone, deleted the messages, and reached across the table to set the phone next to his plate. Then I pulled back and promptly spilled my entire glass of wine in my lap.

"Oh no!" I cried, jumping up. "My suit… I'll be right back."

Ignoring Lannister's offer to help me get out of my clothes, I made a beeline for the restroom at the back of the restaurant. I was almost there, just about to barrel into the women's bathroom, when someone grabbed me by the arm.

I jumped and nearly let out a startled cry but swallowed it when I turned and stared into the flashing blue eyes of Luc Riveaux.

CHAPTER 8

LUC

"**W**HAT THE HELL do you think you're doing?" I demanded as I practically dragged Arianna out the back door of the restaurant.

"Luc, let go." She jerked her arm from my grip and glared at me as she rubbed at her biceps. "That's unacceptable."

I held my hands up in a surrender motion, feeling like a first-class a-hole. "Sorry. I didn't mean to hurt you. But you can't go back in there. Do you have any idea who that guy is?"

"Yes." Her tone was defiant.

Shock hit me in the gut. I stared at her lovely face, the rest of the world fading away around me. My blood ran cold. "You know who he is and yet you're out on a date with him?" I asked, keeping my tone low and very controlled. "Why? And what's with the wig?"

She glanced back at the door, her hands clenched together at her chest. She blew out a breath, and it was then I noticed the slight shaking. "Can we get out of here?"

I nodded once and held my hand out to her, being very careful to not lose my shit. I'd been close when I'd seen them together.

She hesitated for just a moment but then tightened her fingers around mine and let me guide her out to the street. We took the first right turn, and within moments I was helping her into my red Ford F-150.

I climbed into the driver's side, and without

saying a word, I fired the engine and took off down the narrow street.

She pulled the wig off, letting her locks fall softly around her face, and stuffed it under the seat. Then she turned and stared out the window, ignoring me.

It wasn't until I was on the expressway headed south out of New Orleans that she spoke. "How did you know where I was?"

I gritted my teeth to keep from lashing out at her. She'd been on what looked like a date with Lannister. The bastard who'd not only been terrorizing Skye but had also been giving our pack hell for the past few years just because we existed. He was a worthless piece-of-shit bigot who deserved everything he had coming to him. "I asked my cousin Wren to keep an eye on you. He's a chef at one of the restaurants in the Garden District. The pack was concerned you'd become the next target. We never dreamed you'd deliberately go on a date with that cock-sucker."

That last bit came out harsher than I intended. But fuck. What the hell was she doing with him?

"I wasn't dating him. God, Luc. Is that really what you think of me?" She glared at me, and when I didn't respond, she let out a loud huff and stared straight ahead. "You didn't have to come after me. I was doing just fine."

The hell she was. Two weeks ago she hadn't known shifters even existed. Now she was smack in the middle of a showdown between my pack and the Hunters. "You're in danger, Arianna, whether you know it or not."

"I'm not an idiot. Why the hell do you think I was there? Oh, that's right. You think I'd go and date someone who smacked around one of my best friends." She scowled at me, her hands shaking with anger.

"No," I shot back. "That's not what I believe at all. Or at least I don't want to, but you sure haven't given me any reasonable answers as to why you let that slime put his hands on you, so my imagination is running wild."

Fuck. I was shaking too.

She let out another huff and wiped at her shirt. For the first time I noticed it was wet, as if she'd spilled something. And that her lacy bra was visible on the right side, giving me a hint of what I already knew was hiding under that suit. My stomach tightened as I remembered grazing her soft breast with my teeth.

"Where are you taking me?" she asked, startling me out of my demented haze.

"Out of the city. Lannister's going to be looking for you. Asking questions. And if he figures out who you are..." I pressed down on the gas and swerved into another lane, passing a line of cars.

"I know."

"You know? And yet after everything you've been through, you still decided it was a good idea to mess with him?" What the hell was going on with her?

She turned slowly, eyeing me with suspicion. "Skye told you my history?"

I gave her a short nod and consciously softened my tone. "Yes. Not all of it, but enough."

"And?"

I glanced from the road to her hardened features. "And what? You were dealt an awful hand early on in your life. But you've managed to come out of it strong and mostly whole." My mind shot back to the image of her sitting across from Lannister, making my vision cloud with anger. "And brave."

When she didn't answer, I took a deep breath and asked, "Want to tell me what was going on back there?"

She turned her body toward me, finally giving me her full attention. "Not really. But you're going to find out sooner or later anyway."

I exited the freeway and headed south. "I'm all ears."

"Not until we get to wherever we're going. I don't want to do this in the car."

I nodded, made a split-second decision, and took a hard right. The truck barreled down a two-lane highway toward the edge of the bayou.

"Where are you taking me?" Arianna said, clutching the door.

"Here." I turned at the sign that read Hidden Bayou. The truck bounced over the dirt road. I knew without looking at Arianna that her anxiety had heightened. I could smell it in the air. "Relax," I said lightly and pulled to a stop in front of a tidy Creole cottage. "The cabins belong to my cousins. We can talk here."

She slowly let go of the door handle and glanced around. "Your cousins? Are they shifters too?"

"Yeah." I chuckled and jumped out of the truck. When I opened her door for her, I asked, "You didn't think my brothers and I were the only ones did you?"

"Of course not. I just… You guys never talked about them." She climbed down and frowned when the fine dust from the dirt road soiled her high heels.

I took her hand and led her toward the main entrance. "Jace and Silas had a falling-out a few years back. It's a sore subject."

"About what?"

I stopped midstep and glanced down at her. "My father's death. Silas was there when it happened."

Her fingers tightened around mine. "I'm sorry. Was he… I mean, how?"

"Shot. An old rival of his got him in the head. There was no coming back." That empty feeling I was used to getting when I spoke about what had happened to my dad failed to come. And all I had inside me was regret. Regret that we'd lost him so early, that I'd been too cocky to listen to him when he gave advice, that I'd never really understood him.

"I'm so sorry, Luc. That's awful." She leaned into me, hugging me with one arm. She felt so nice, so perfect, and I just stood there, my arms wrapped around her, not caring what she'd done earlier or why. All that mattered was she was in my arms again. Where she belonged.

"Luc?" A door slammed.

I glanced over Arianna's head and spotted Silas. He was bigger than I remembered, as if he'd been hitting the gym hard. He had more tattoos as well. Both arms had been completely sleeved.

"Silas." I nodded. "Long time no see."

Arianna dropped her hold on me and held out a hand. "Hello. I'm Arianna."

He took her hand and very politely said, "It's a pleasure to meet you. I'm Silas, the black sheep of the family."

She smiled and cast a glance down his body. "I think the image probably works for you."

My wolf rose up and I let out an involuntary growl.

Arianna turned her big eyes on me, her eyebrows raised in surprise.

Silas laughed and said to her, "I guess we know who you belong to."

"Belong?" The incredulity in her tone

would've made a mere mortal uncertain, but my wolf had already made up his mind.

I took a step and draped my arm around her shoulder and said to her, "Yes. As far as Silas is concerned, you're mine."

"I don't belong—"

Silas let out an amused huff of laughter. "Good luck with this one, Lucas. Looks like she's going to have to be dragged kicking and screaming."

I shook my head. "It's not like that."

"The hell it's not. I give you three days. You won't last longer than that." He turned to Arianna. "It's easier if you don't fight it, but it's not nearly as fun."

"I beg your pardon?" she asked, shifting her gaze between the pair of us.

"Cut it out, Silas," I ordered. "Listen, do you have a free cabin we could use for a couple of hours? We have things to discuss."

"Discuss," he said with a fair amount of innuendo in his tone. "Sure. Cabin four in the back is open. Take all the time you need. Let me know when you're done so we can get housekeeping in to change the sheets."

I didn't bother to correct him as he strode off to his Jeep.

Arianna glared at me. "He thinks we're here for an afternoon quickie."

I laughed. "I highly doubt he thinks there's going to be anything quick about it."

"Luc!" She stood beside me, her hands balled on her hips, her chin jutting out. "That's not funny."

"You're right," I said, sobering. "There's nothing funny about what happened today. I need to know exactly what you were doing and why."

She clamped her lips together. "When we get to the cabin."

CHAPTER 9

ARIANNA

ON THE OUTSIDE, the cabin was old, rustic, and somewhat shabby-looking. Paint peeled from the porch railings. Unruly vines crawled up the side of the house. The entire structure appeared to be leaning to one side. "They rent these out?" I asked, somewhat horrified.

"Yes. It's not that bad. Come on." He strode up the surprisingly solid porch steps and opened the door for me.

I peeked inside, my eyes going wide. It was gorgeous. Cedar planks lined the walls and the open beam ceiling. A small, upscale kitchen took up one wall, and off to the side was a master bedroom and bathroom suite that rivaled even the poshest hotels. "Oh my god. It's lovely. Why does the outside look so terrible?"

"It's that way on purpose. To show what the area looked like one hundred years ago. They bill it as authentic luxury."

"And that works?"

"It appears so."

I took my shoes off and left them near the front door so as not to track dirt into the pristine cabin. "I can't believe how nice this is."

Luc nodded. "Silas is a contractor. He does this for a living."

"Not run the cabins?" I asked.

He shook his head. "The three of them own this place, but Hannah runs it. She's Wren's stepsister. Complicated family dynamic."

"I see."

"Come on. Let's sit down." He waved me over to the couch, but I sat in the chair, feeling like I needed a little space in order to confess what I'd done.

He took the end of the couch and stared at me expectantly.

Shit. How was I supposed to start? Just rip the Band-Aid off? No. Too harsh. He needed background info first.

"Arianna?"

"I know. I'm collecting my thoughts."

The muscle in his jaw twitched, but then he visibly forced himself to relax. "Just tell me," he said, his tone deliberately patient. "Whatever it is."

"Fine." I took a deep breath, let it out, and stared him in the eye. "I assume Skye told you I don't have family."

He nodded. "Yes, and that you left your foster family behind after you graduated high school."

"Right. Except I do have a foster brother I talk to. He's the only one. He also, uh… Well, let's just say he's self-employed."

Luc raised both eyebrows. "Illegal?"

"Yeah."

"Drugs?" His tone was harsh, full of judgment.

"No!" Dammit. I had to just tell him. My heart started hammering. "He's a world-class hacker, and I hired him to scrub that video Lannister has. That's why I was with him today. I put an app on his phone that will allow my brother to infiltrate all his passwords, clouds, e-mail, etc. Once it's gone, your pack will be free."

Luc's expression went blank, then a flash of anger settled over his features before disappearing again.

"Listen. I couldn't sit back and let that ass-hole get away with his bullshit, knowing I could do something about it. So you can be upset if you want to, but I'd do a lot more than that to keep you and Skye safe." There. I'd said it.

Luc stood up and I half expected him to walk out. I don't know why I thought that. Maybe because it's what I always did when things got hard. But then he kneeled in front of me and took my hands in his. "Tell me one thing."

My insides turned to mush at his gentle tone. "If I can."

"Why did you leave without saying good-bye last week?"

My heart dropped to my stomach, making me queasy.

"I need to know." His eyes were intense,

searching mine as if his next move depended entirely on my answer.

Now was my moment. If I ever wanted to get past my fear of trusting the people I cared about, if I ever wanted to try to open up again, this was my chance. I squeezed his fingers, needing to hold on to him, to make sure he stayed after I spoke my truth.

"I needed you to think I didn't care about you," I whispered.

A storm rolled through his eyes. "Why?"

"Because…" I cleared my throat, hating that I sounded so weak. Steeling myself, I forced the words out in a strong voice. "I was afraid of the world you live in. And I thought if I let myself stay any longer, I'd never leave."

He frowned, disappointment registering in his gaze. But then he jerked his head up. "Was? What does that mean? That you're not afraid now?"

I gave him a tiny smile. "Oh, Luc. I'm terrified. But it didn't take me long to realize that doesn't matter. I care about you. More than I wanted to. More than I thought possible, really. And if I go on living a *safe* life, I'm not going to be living at all."

"There's no denying you're safer staying away from me and my pack." Pain laced his words.

I eased one of my hands out of his and cupped his cheek. "I think you're wrong. Look at what you've already done for me. You had someone keep an eye on me, and as soon as they saw I was in trouble, you came for me."

"I came to kill that son of a bitch," he growled.

"No you didn't," I said softly.

"I wanted to."

"No doubt. But in the end all you did was protect me. To be honest, with all the shady people I've known in my past, the place I feel safest is with you. And if I haven't completely blown it, I think I'd like to spend some more time on your bayou."

His breath caught. Then he stood up, pulling me with him. We faced each other, tension and longing sparking between us. "How much time?"

I reached up and barely brushed my lips over his. "As long as you've got."

CHAPTER 10

LUC

SOMETHING INSIDE ME shattered. That part of my heart that I'd hardened, that I'd thought had turned to stone. Love and need and passion gripped me, and I pulled her into my arms, determined to make her mine. "I want you, Arianna."

She let out a breath she'd been holding. "I want you too. More than you know."

"No." I shook my head, certain she hadn't understood. "I want you forever. To be mine and only mine."

Her eyes went wide as shock filtered over

her face. "Are you saying, um, that you want me to…"

"Be my mate, Arianna. If you'll have me." Everything inside me tensed. After years of denying myself even the thought of bonding with someone, suddenly it was all I wanted. For better or worse. Even if the worst happened and it wasn't forever. It was enough for now. My heart thundered while I waited for her response.

"But… why?" Her voice was earnest, as if she really needed to know in order to answer me.

I took a step forward, closing the distance between us. "So many reasons. You're brave. Strong. Loyal. Smart. Sassy. Confident." Leaning down, I brushed my lips over the pulse pounding in her neck. Then I whispered, "And I want you so fucking much it hurts."

"Oh God," she breathed.

I buried one hand in her thick hair and scraped my teeth down her long neck.

She shivered and arched into me.

"Tell me what you want, Arianna."

She moved one arm up, slipping her hand around my neck. Her other hand rested on my hip. "You," she said and kissed me, her lips moving over mine with sudden fervor.

I groaned and shoved my tongue into her mouth, tasting her as I pushed her against the wall. My body went stiff with need. I wanted her. All of her. But I broke off suddenly and took a step back.

"What's wrong?" she asked, confusion tainting her lustful eyes.

Reaching out, I took her hand in mine and flattened it against my chest over my heart. "You have me already, Ari. Before we go any further, I need to know if I have you. All of you."

Her mouth worked, unable to get the words out. Tears shone in her lovely dark eyes, but she was smiling. Then she nodded.

Fear and elation mixed, nearly bringing me to my knees. "That's a yes?" I forced out.

She took a step right into my arms and in a shaky voice said, "Yes. You have me. Make me your mate."

I was frozen in that moment as I watched her bright eyes, love pouring from her. Felt as if the world had suddenly opened up and given me a gift I'd craved but always thought I'd never deserved. I brushed her hair to the side, trailing my fingers over her soft skin. "There's no going back."

She nodded and reached for the edge of my T-shirt, pulling it up and over my head. Staring at me, she traced her fingers over the wolf I'd had tattooed on my ribcage. "I know. Make me yours. Now."

The words rippled through me, breaking down the last of my barriers. And something warm and wonderful filled my heart as emotion nearly choked me. I forced a swallow and stilled her hands.

Her fingers twined with mine as she gazed up at me, her lips turned up in a sexy little smile. "Make love to me, Luc."

She didn't have to ask twice. In one swift movement, I reached down and picked her up, cradling her to my chest.

She giggled. "This isn't necessary."

"Trust me. It is." I pressed a kiss to her temple and strode into the bedroom where I placed her carefully back on her feet. Then I claimed her lips once more, only this time I was tender, gentle, as I pushed her suit jacket off, leaving her in the white button-down shirt.

My wolf wanted to rip it off her, claim her as quickly as possible. But the man in me had other plans. I kissed my way down her neck while simultaneously undoing the buttons. And when I'd freed her of the shirt, I brushed my fingers over the swell of her ample breast. "I've never seen anyone as beautiful as you."

She gazed at me with intensity, her body taut under my touch. "You're not so bad yourself," she said, breathless.

I smiled and undid the clasp at the front of her bra, baring her to me. "And these"—I took one nipple in my mouth, teasing it with my tongue before I let it go and glanced up—"are a masterpiece of perfection."

She opened her mouth to say something, but I pulled the other one into my mouth and nibbled gently, making her suck in a sharp breath of air.

"Oh," was all she managed to get out. Her breath came in short hitches, her eyes closed, her body yielding to me. She was so warm, so pliable, so fucking perfect.

Mine.

My wolf was just beneath the surface, ready to take her. I forced him back, taking my time as I undid her pants and pushed them, along with her black silk panties, off her curvy hips. The shadows from the afternoon sun filtered in, illuminating her bare body.

"Glorious," I said and lifted her up to lay her on the bed.

Her eyes sparkled and her lips curved as she swept her gaze over me. "Lose the jeans, wolf," she ordered.

My heart twisted and the animal inside me let out a silent roar of approval. I gave her what I knew was my wolfish smile and tore the rest of my clothes off.

She quirked one eyebrow, leisurely assessing the goods. "Impressive."

"You ain't seen nothin' yet," I promised.

Both of her eyebrows shot straight up. "You're telling me this is going to be hotter than last time, because—"

"You have no idea." I lowered myself over her and onto the bed. "I'm going to show you exactly what it means to say you're making love."

"Kiss me. Here," she said and touched her lower lip.

I bent my head and took her lip between mine, sucking gently as my hands cupped her heavy breasts.

She buried her fingers in my hair, her body already yielding to me. She was glorious. And I wanted to taste her everywhere. Know every inch of her. I moved from her mouth to her neck, down past the valley of her cleavage, to her stomach and lower.

"Luc," she said, arching up and opening her legs for me.

Perfect.

I took my time, kissing her hip, the back of her knees, running my fingers from her ankles to her inner thighs, making her shiver with my light touch. Exploring everywhere except the one spot I knew she wanted most.

"Luc," she moaned. "You're driving me insane."

I let out a low chuckle.

"Touch me. Please."

"Not yet," I said and lowered my head to blow on her sex.

Her hips jerked and she clutched the bedspread.

I darted my tongue out, licking and tasting her inner thigh as I splayed my hand over her abdomen.

She was trembling, wired with passion. Exactly the way I wanted her.

"So lovely," I said and dipped my tongue into her center.

Her entire body shuddered.

This is what it was to love her. To explore every inch of her, to mark her with my touch.

Mine.

She was so sweet and hot, her hips writhing with each stroke of my tongue. And when she gasped for air, her breathing out of control, I lifted my head and kissed my way up her body, stopping when I got just below her ear. "You're gorgeous, Ari."

"And you're maddening," she said, wrapping her legs around me. Her hips jerked up and she ground into me. "I need you."

Pleasure rippled through me at the first feel of her slick heat against my cock.

"Now," she demanded, her fingernails digging into my back.

I was lost, plunging into her, hard and deep.

"Oh!" she cried out, rising up to meet me thrust for thrust.

The man in me fled and the wolf took over, devouring her as I scraped my teeth down her neck and lifted one leg higher, thrusting hard and deep and fast.

"Yes, Luc. God, yes!" Her movements matched mine with each punishing stroke.

And then suddenly, with a strength I hadn't known she possessed, she rolled us over and rode me hard.

Holy fuck. I reared up, holding her waist with one arm while I relentlessly sucked her right breast, undoubtedly bruising her tender flesh.

"Oh God, oh God, oh God," she cried out as her muscles tensed around me.

I tore my mouth away from her breast and said, "Yes. Mine." And then as she came apart, I bit down hard on her neck and made her my mate.

CHAPTER II
ARIANNA

I WOKE IN the early light before dawn. Luc had insisted we stay at the cabin for the night because every shifter transition was different. There was no telling how a person would take it.

I was lucky. I had barely noticed it at all, except for the insane connection Luc and I now shared. It was as if he was a part of me. I could feel his presence in a way I couldn't before. It was disconcerting yet comforting at the same time.

He'd said it was my wolf communicating with his. A pack thing. And that I'd get used to it.

I already was. Snuggling into him, my heart melted. He'd taken such care of me through the night, always checking to be sure I was all right, staring at me with emotion-filled eyes. It was unlike anything I'd experienced before. To be honest, it scared the shit out of me. But my wolf was content, and that feeling inside me actually kept me calm and nestled beside him. The urge to run was gone.

Closing my eyes, I breathed him in, my heart swelling with love.

Luc's arm tightened around me, and I was on the verge of falling back to sleep when his phone started to ring.

He bolted upright and grabbed it. "What?"

I sat up, clutching the sheet to my naked body.

Luc put a possessive hand on my thigh and

said into the phone, "We're on our way."

He ended the call. "We have to get back to the bar. Jace spotted Lannister's people near Grandfather's place about twenty minutes ago."

I sat there in the bed, frozen as Luc pulled his jeans on.

"Arianna?"

I jerked my head up. "Yes?"

"We have to hurry."

The urgency in his tone propelled me out of the bed. "Of course."

Luc was dressed and had his boots on before I even made it to the bathroom. "I'll be right back," he said and strode out of the room. The door slammed behind him a few seconds later.

I hurried to pull on my sexy business suit and longed for my capris and a T-shirt. Maybe Skye would have something I could borrow.

"Arianna?" Luc called from the other room.

I hurried out and found him standing in the door, holding a white paper bag and two coffees. My stomach rumbled and I shot him a grateful smile. I was starving.

"Ready?" he asked.

"Yep."

He handed me the bag and a cup and led me out to his truck. A Jeep was parked next to it, Silas and two other tall men standing there.

"Morning," Silas said, a sly smile on his face. "Welcome to the family."

Oh, jeez. They all knew what we'd been up to the night before. My face heated.

"Arianna, meet Darien and Wren. You remember Silas from yesterday, right?"

"Sure." I nodded to the men, who grunted a greeting before climbing into the Jeep.

"They're coming with us," Luc said, opening the truck door for me.

I glanced over to see Silas getting into the driver's seat of the Jeep. "Does Jace know?"

"Nope."

"This is going to be interesting," I said, remembering Luc had mentioned Silas and Jace hadn't spoken in years.

"That's one way of putting it." Luc fired up the truck and sped down the dirt road and onto the two-lane highway.

Forty minutes later, we pulled into the parking lot of Wolves of the Rising Sun. Rayna was pacing the porch, her long dark hair pulled into a high ponytail.

She jumped off the top step and stalked over to the truck, intercepting Luc as he slammed his door shut. "Where the hell have you been?"

He jerked his head in my direction. "With Ari."

I gave her a little wave.

Surprise lit her dark eyes, followed by genuine shock. "She's your mate." Staring up at Luc, she shook her head in disbelief. "I can't believe it."

He held his arm out to me, tucking me close to his side. "Yes you can. Where are Aiden and Jace?"

"They're out on the water, keeping an eye on the crew."

"I thought you guys were going to clear the field," I said to Luc.

"We were going to, but just as we were about to get started, we got slammed with tours. And with the bar being rebuilt, we couldn't afford to turn them away."

I nodded, not sure what to say. I was both relieved and disappointed. I wanted it gone, but I didn't want them to be the ones to clear it. I checked my phone. No messages. Damn. My brother was supposed to text me after he was done scrubbing Lannister's phone and computer for the video.

Rayna glanced past us at the Jeep that had just turned into the parking lot. We all watched as Silas parked next to Luc's truck.

"What are they doing here?" Rayna asked.

"We need back up," Luc said.

She shook her head. "Jace is going to shit a brick."

"He'll get over it." Luc glanced down at me and my outfit. Then he handed me his keys. "Here. Take the truck and go back to my place. I'll meet you there after we take care of this."

"What?" I scowled. "You've got to be kidding me. I'm not going to sit and wait in your house. I'm going with you."

Luc gazed down at me, his expression torn.

Rayna snorted and held a hand out to me.

"Never mind him. He's just got a giant case of male ego getting in his way. Come on. I've got a change of clothes in the car."

She retrieved a duffel bag and waved for me to follow her into the bar. I was grateful for the shorts, tank top, and tennis shoes, and although I could've used a little more coverage, at least I wasn't in the business suit.

When we got back outside, Luc and his cousins were waiting for us on one of the airboats. His brothers and Skye had already taken off. Just as we joined them, I got a text from Smoke. *It's done. All the threads have been hunted down and deleted. No more blackmail.*

Thank you. I owe you one, I typed back.

Not one. Several. Cash only.

I smiled at that, although I knew he wasn't kidding. Smoke didn't work for free. I turned to tell Luc, but he was in the driver's seat and the motor turned over, drowning out the opportunity to say anything.

It didn't matter now anyway. Once the Riveauxs had the situation under control, we could call the authorities and that would be that.

Luc maneuvered the boat through the bayou with the skill of a man who'd lived his life on the water, and within minutes he was gliding the boat to a stop beside an identical one. There was no dock, just a rope that was tied off to a large tree.

"Where are we?" I asked Rayna when the engine cut out.

"The back of the island. We had to stop somewhere they wouldn't hear us."

I nodded and grimaced at the thought of walking through the overgrown vegetation. My bare legs were going to suffer something awful.

The men filed off the boat, and as soon as their feet hit solid ground, they started stripping.

"Whoa," I said in a hushed tone to Luc. "What are they doing?"

"Shifting," he said with a chuckle.

"Right." I glanced away, uncomfortable watching them bare themselves.

Rayna laughed. "Newbie." Then she stepped out of her shorts and stripped down. Within moments she had changed into a gorgeous brindle wolf and took off after Silas and his brothers.

A tingle sparked and grew in my gut, my limbs suddenly heavy. "Luc?" I forced out through aching jaws.

"Shit," he said. "You're shifting."

"Huh?" I glanced down at myself, but my head spun and I had to close my eyes.

Luc worked fast, divesting me of my borrowed clothes, but I barely registered it. Everything hurt. Bones cracked. Pain seized my muscles. My form contorted, and then suddenly I was standing on four paws, the scents of the bayou magnified. Mud, cedar, and the pungent stench of moss and mold filled my senses.

Something nudged me and I jerked, snarling.

Luc danced away and back again, rubbing his wolf head against mine.

Mate.

The word was my only coherent thought as I chased after him into the tall grass. My paws hit the damp earth, and although everything was new and foreign, it was also right. Like I belonged. I felt free. Wild. Unstoppable.

Joy filled my soul as everything but the feeling of being a wolf faded away. I had no cognition of why we'd come to the island or where we were going. It didn't matter. I was a wolf. Born to run.

And then it happened. A bullet whizzed by me, barely missing before it slammed into a tree. I froze and stared up into the eyes of a man holding a rifle. His eyes burned with glee as he aimed right for me.

A growl came from my left, and then I was knocked to the side just as another shot rang out. I rolled and sprang up on my paws, my teeth bared, ready to fight.

Laughter filled the clearing. "Got one!" someone shouted.

I swiveled my head, scanning the area, but I knew before I spotted him. The connection I'd felt all day had vanished.

Luc!

I let out a long howl and then nudged him with my nose. He didn't move.

Something broke inside. Some restraint that was connected to my humanity.

The snap of a twig caught my attention and I spun, staring right into the business end of a rifle. It didn't matter. I was too far gone to care what happened to me. I charged, wrapping my jaws around the steel barrel. With one shake of my head, I pulled the rifle from the gunman's hand. Dropping it, I lunged, vaguely aware of shouts and snarling coming from a few feet away. I ignored everything, had one mission. Kill the bastard who'd shot my mate.

I dug my paws into the man's chest, and on instinct went for his throat. He thrashed and I caught him in the shoulder.

His cries fell on deaf ears.

My victim writhed in pain beneath me. I clamped down tighter, determined to rip him apart.

More shouts, followed by howls of wolves I inherently knew were my pack.

I was oblivious to all of it. My world had narrowed to the gunman.

He stilled, going limp beneath me. Triumph filled me and I loosened my hold, only to have my victim rear up in a surprising display of strength and clock me in the head. I rolled, dazed from the impact. But my agile body still managed to instinctually land upright, the gunman only a few feet from me.

And this time when I lunged, I caught him by the neck, my teeth tearing through his skin like rice paper.

"Arianna!" Luc's voice filtered through my bloodlust. "Stop. It's over."

That beautiful sound of his voice was like a call to my soul. He'd survived. I let go and slowly backed off the lifeless form.

"Come here," Luc said, coaxing me to his side. I shuffled over to him, spitting the taste of blood out of my mouth.

He'd shifted and stood naked in the moonlight, blood seeping from a wound in his chest.

I whined and nudged his hand, noticing for the first time all his cousins, still in wolf form, were spread out in a half circle, watching us.

"I need you to shift, Ari. I need to make sure you're okay," Luc said, his voice shallow as if he was having trouble breathing.

It was enough to force my shift. I had to tend to him, hold him. Get him to a hospital. Within moments I stood in front of him, naked and shaking from the adrenaline rush. "You're hurt," I said, pressing my hand to his wound.

He pulled me into his arms and hugged me tight. Tighter than a man who'd just been shot should've been able to. "I'll be fine. Are you?"

I nodded into his shoulder. "I thought you… Holy balls. I lost our connection."

"The bullet put me unconscious for a few minutes before my body started to heal," he said into my hair. "It's going to take a lot more than that to take me down."

I pulled back and eyed the blood seeping between my fingers. "God, Luc. You're losing a lot of blood. We need to get you out of here."

"Not without the others. Jace, Skye, Aiden, and Rayna are still out there."

"But—"

He pressed his fingers to my lips. "It heals when I shift. I'd have already done it again, but I was worried about you." He cast a glance at the unconscious guy laying a few feet away. "You could've killed him."

Shame and horror washed over me. "That was my goal," I whispered, my voice so low I wasn't sure he heard it.

He nodded. "It's the wolf. Not your fault."

Of course it was, but I didn't say that. He needed to shift to stop the bleeding, and the longer we stood there, the more blood he'd lose. "I'm fine. Shift. Do what you have to do."

Luc gave me a quick kiss on the temple and then fell to his knees and shifted. My wolf followed, tugged under by the newly restored connection.

Luc took a step and nudged me, his form of saying hello as a wolf, I guessed, and then jerked his head, indicating it was time to go. I had no choice but to trust he was well enough and took off after him.

The four males ran in a formation around me, clearly playing the role of protectors. And as far as I was concerned, that was fine. After my attack on the gunman, I wasn't eager to get into another altercation.

The scent of the grow site overpowered everything, and the pack slowed as we took our time navigating around it.

We came into the clearing, and Silas went ahead while Luc stayed by my side.

We each crept forward, keeping our heads down so as not to be seen. But when we poked our heads out of the tall grass, I was shocked to see Jace and Skye standing there talking to a man in a DEA jacket, his badge flashing.

Holy shit. I glanced at Luc. He shook his head and jerked it to the left.

I followed his gaze, noting a group of five individuals all handcuffed and on their knees. They'd been apprehended, and Jace was shaking the agent's hand.

Clearly the situation was under control. Aiden backed up, slipping once again into the brush. His cousins and Rayna appeared from the cover of the trees and the six of us took off back to the airboat.

CHAPTER 12

ARIANNA

EVERYTHING ACHED. My arms, legs, head. Luc said my transformation was catching up with me. I needed sleep. And food. None of which I could get at the bar where we were currently congregated.

He was impatient to get me home, and after what seemed like hours of the same bullshit questions, he stood and held his hand out to me. "We're leaving."

Jace jerked his head up, his eyes narrowed.

"I'll walk you out," one of the agents said. The one who'd been taking notes but hadn't said a word all morning.

"Fine," Luc said, agitation in his tone.

I leaned into him, exhausted. It had been one hell of a twenty-four hours.

"You're Arianna, right?" the agent said once we were outside.

I nodded, too tired to care what he wanted. "Yeah."

"I have something for you. It's from Smoke." He held out a small cream-colored envelope.

"What?" I took the envelope, my body going numb with fear. Oh God. They'd caught him. "Where is he?"

He smiled reassuringly. "At home, I suspect. He deserves a day off."

I stared at him dumfounded. "What does that mean? He doesn't have a job."

"Actually, he does. With the FBI. After you asked him for help, he got in touch and fed us the information we needed to take down this ring. That guy who's been hassling y'all, Lannister? He was taken into custody last night. So thank you. But next time? You can just give us a call. We're not the enemy."

I gaped at him, too shocked to process. "Smoke works for the FBI?"

He nodded. "It's confidential information, but it was part of the deal he made with me when he gave us the tip. He didn't want to keep this secret from you any longer. He's been on the payroll for five years. Obviously he's undercover."

"Holy shit." Years of frustration and worry melted away as I stared at the agent in amazement. "He's not a criminal?"

The agent shrugged and his smile widened. "It depends on who you ask. But as far as the federal government is concerned, no."

I turned to Luc, tears stinging my eyes. "I can't believe it."

He put his arm around me and hugged me to him.

"Just keep it under wraps, all right?" he said to Luc. "I know you boys are good at that sort of thing. We've kept your secret. I'd appreciate it if you did the same." He gave me a slight nod and took off across the parking lot.

Both Luc and I stood straighter as we watched him slip into his nondescript black sedan.

"He knows," Luc said. "About our existence."

I stared up at him. "Is that a problem?"

He shook his head. "No. Not as long as he's good for his word. I just don't know how he knows."

The bar door swung open and Jace and Silas

came storming out.

Neither of them said anything as they stalked over to Silas's Jeep. Darien and Wren followed but waited with us on the porch.

"What's going on?" Luc asked them.

Darien shrugged. "They're either coming to an agreement or they're going to kill each other."

Luc closed his eyes and took a deep breath. "Christ." Then he looked down at me. "Ready to go home?"

I nodded and followed him to his truck. As we left the parking lot, Jace threw the first punch.

I grimaced.

Luc laughed. "It's about time."

"That's how they're going to work it out?"

"Yep. Either that or kill each other. Both will end the feud."

I shook my head. "Men."

"Wolves," he corrected.

I chuckled. Nothing about my life would ever be normal again. My smiled widened at the thought, joy filling my soul. Life might not be normal, but it sure as hell was going to be exciting. I scooted over to the middle of the truck and placed a hand on Luc's thigh. "Take me home. I'm ready for bed."

He arched an eyebrow. "I thought you were tired."

I leaned in, kissing his shoulder. "I was. Now all I want is you."

Heat flashed in his eyes. And then he hit the gas, breaking about half a dozen traffic laws as he raced home.

CHAPTER 13

LUC

Three weeks later

THE BAR WAS packed for the grand reopening. Rayna and Aiden were behind the bar, flirting up a storm as always. Jace was upselling the top-shelf booze to everyone and their brother. Skye was holding court in her booth with her model friends again. And every townie within forty miles was packed into the newly remodeled space.

Just about the only thing that was different was that our cousins were here. And every single woman in the bar was staring at Silas and some of the taken ones too. Only he didn't seem to notice. He was sitting at a booth by himself, drinking whiskey, neat, while his brothers co-zied up with Skye and her friends. Can't say I blamed them. I'd done the same thing over a month ago.

I glanced over at Arianna. She had on a tank top, short shorts, and cowboy boots. Fucking sexy. She smiled at me from her place up on the makeshift stage. Tonight was karaoke night according to her and Skye. And Arianna was the first victim.

Rayna handed me a couple of whiskeys and jerked her head toward Silas. "Go talk to him."

"He looks like he wants to be left alone."

She rolled her eyes. "Men are so dense. If that were true, he'd never have come in to-night."

I shook my head. "If you know so much,

why don't you go talk to him?"

"I would, but someone has to pour the drinks."

Her pointed tone didn't go unnoticed. When the bar was busy and they were all working, they never failed to mention I wasn't. Except I worked more hours than all of them, taking care of the paperwork and accounting for both businesses when I wasn't running tours. "You do realize I work during the day when you and Aiden are… uh, sleeping, right?"

Her smile turned to a wicked grin. "Sleeping. Right."

"Christ. Just stop. I'm going." I laughed, grabbed the drinks, and headed over to my sulking cousin. Sitting down, I slid one of the glasses over to him. "Why aren't you over there taking that blonde from Wren? She's been eye-fucking you all night."

His lips twitched. "Too easy."

I nodded. "All right, what about her friend? The redhead with the nice rack."

"Darien has his eye on her." He shrugged. "I'm not interested anyway."

I turned and glanced at the table full of beauties. "Seriously?"

"Seriously." He picked up the whiskey, downed it, and then stood. "I'm leaving. Tell your brothers congratulations on the reopening."

"Will do." I sat in the booth, watching him make his way to the door.

The music started up, and Arianna's soulful voice filled the bar. Jesus, everything about her was gorgeous and turned me on. If I made it through her rendition of the Adele song without carrying her off the stage, it would be a miracle.

Trying my best to curb my libido, I turned away from Arianna just in time to see Hannah

Thorne walk through the front door and straight into Silas. She stumbled but he reached out, steadying her.

Then their eyes met. And suddenly I knew why Silas wasn't interested in Skye's friends. He was in love with a girl who was completely off-limits—his half brother's stepsister.

Holy fuck. I glanced back at Wren and grimaced. The normally easygoing Davenne brother was already on his feet, his fists clenched.

I slid to the edge of the seat, ready to intervene, but before anyone else could move, Silas lifted Hannah up, turned, and removed her from his path. They stared at each other for another beat, then he clasped his hand over the back of his neck and left without saying a word to her.

"She looks like an angel," Arianna said, pushing me over as she slid into the booth next to me.

"And he looks like the devil in disguise."

She laughed. "That's why she wants him."

"If you say so." I turned to her, my body heating with instant desire.

"Stop looking at me like that," she said, a flush covering her cheeks.

"Like what?"

"Like you're going to make me come right here in the booth."

"I'm game if you are."

Desire flashed in her gorgeous eyes, and I thought for a minute she was considering it. But then she said, "If we leave right now, will they miss us?"

"Probably."

"Do we care?"

"Nope." I nudged her out of the booth. "Let's go, mate. I have work to do."

She let out a huff of laughter. "Anyone ever

tell you you're a workaholic?"

I grinned. "It's why you love me."

"Just one of the many reasons," she said coyly.

"Let's see. Once in the shower. Twice on the bed. Then the kitchen counter. And if we want to get technical, the kitchen table. That's five already today. How many more reasons do you need?"

"Let's make it double or nothing." She winked and sauntered out the front door, her ass moving with an exaggerated sway.

"You've got your hands full with that one," Wren said from behind me.

"You have no idea." Then I strode out, my heart full and my libido firmly out of control. Just the way Arianna liked it.

Sign up for Kenzie's newsletter at www.kenziecox.com to be notified of new releases. Do you prefer text messages? Sign up for text alerts! Just text SHIFTERSROCK to 24587 to register.

Book List:

<u>Wolves of the Rising Sun</u>

Jace

Aiden

Luc

Craved

Silas

Darien

Wren

Printed in Great Britain
by Amazon